Taking a Chance

by Becky Monson

BOOKS BY BECKY MONSON

Thirty-Two Going on Spinster
Thirty-Three Going on Girlfriend
Thirty-Four Going on Bride
Speak Now or Forever Hold You Peace

CONNECT WITH BECKY
www.beckymonson.com

To Sadie
Who never got a chance to go to the top of the Empire
State Building but is up in the clouds,
watching over us always.

CHAPTER 1

"Are you okay?" the guy next to me asks. At least I think it's a guy; his voice is low enough. I can't seem to look up from the floor to verify. What I can see though, is tan cargo shorts and fairly muscular, hairy calves, so that would lead me to believe he's a dude. Although I've met my share of woman with hairy legs, which is, you know, girl power and all that.

Am I okay? That's a loaded question. Here's the short answer: nope. I am totally *not* okay. You would think by the way I'm holding onto the shiny brass rails he would know that. Maybe it's one of those rhetorical questions. Because honestly, there could be permanent nerve damage to my hands, I'm gripping so tightly. Mind you, if this tiny box-sized deathtrap suddenly fell off its rails and plummeted to the bottom of the building, I doubt my grasp on this railing would do anything to help me survive the crash.

Now why would my brain even go there? I might start hyperventilating. What was it that my Google search last night told me to do? Right. I remember. Look around me and find five things I can see, four things I can touch, three things I can hear, two things I can smell, and one thing I can taste.

Here's the problem with that. When you're on the verge of losing it, you don't have time to do any of those things. Maybe if I just focus on part of it. If I only do half, maybe I'll have half a panic attack. Totally logical. That's just mathematics, right there. Okay, so I'll just skip to two things I can smell. That's easy: body odor, and I'm pretty sure the woman next to me just passed gas. And one thing I can taste: my own bile.

This is not working. I cannot half-ass a panic attack.

"Seriously, are you okay?" cargo shorts he/she asks me.

"Huh?" I pull my eyes up from their focus on the floor, up long legs and a rather lengthy torso, past a nice strong jaw that has a bit of stubble even at this time in the morning, and into a pair of intense brown eyes. Yep, he's for sure a dude. A very good-looking dude, actually, who looks concerned. And he should be—I'm likely to barf on his leather flip-flops at any moment.

Wow, his eyes are chocolaty-brown. Like pools of melted fudge. The contrast against the whites of his eyes is striking. And on closer inspection, the brown is rimmed with gold. I've never seen eyes like that in all my twenty-four years. They're the kind of eyes that make you think of two story colonials with white picket fences, minivans, and babies. My hormones begin chatting amongst themselves; this was far more excitement than they'd seen in a while.

"You okay?" Brown-eyed handsomeness asks again. His eyes change from genuine concern to a more worried look. Because I'm totally ogling. Elena would so mock me if she were here.

Of course, if Elena were here, then I wouldn't be. Which makes me wish even more that she were here. I clear my throat and look away, back down to the floor.

"I think I'm having a nervous breakdown, actually," I say, finally finding the words to reply. Wow, that sounded utterly melodramatic. Elena would *so* be mocking me right now.

Someone in the crowded elevator snickers. I look up from the floor to make sure it wasn't him. It wasn't.

"A nervous breakdown?" he repeats, the corners of his mouth lifting. Is he mocking me? Because if he is, I know exactly where to focus my hurling, if and when I actually do it.

"Yep," I say, and remember to breathe slowly out of my mouth. Google told me taking slow, deep breaths would help. Google, I'm realizing, is a big fat liar.

I close my eyes so the spinning stops. How can a two-minute ride feel like an eternity?

"Ah," he says with an air of Sherlock in his voice, as if he just put all the clues together to figure me out. "Claustrophobia."

"I'm not claustrophobic," I say, although I sort of am. But that's not why I'm freaking out right now.

"Acrophobia?"

"I'm not scared of spiders," I snap, opening my eyes so he can see the annoyance in them. My ocean-colored eyes may not be as striking as his chocolate ones, but they can definitely pack a punch when needed.

He chuckles, unaffected by my glare. "Acrophobia is a fear of heights."

Oh, right. I knew that. So along with hyperventilating, sweaty palms (and let's be honest—pits), and nausea, heights can also cause brain fog.

Yes, I'm afraid of heights. I'm also slightly scared of elevators and crowds. I'm not going to tell him this, though. He'd wonder why I was here in the first place, since that pretty much makes up this entire experience: small spaces, crowds, and heights.

The elevator makes an odd jerking movement and I white-knuckle the handrail, closing my eyes again. Maybe if I close them tight enough, I can wish myself away from this situation. *There's no place like home. There's no place like home.*

"Hey," brown-eyed hot guy says, his voice gentle. "We're almost there." He puts a hand on my shoulder.

Normally, my body would have a full-throttle jump of rejection at his touch. I don't do touch from strangers. I'm not a touchy-feely person even with people I've known my entire life. But for some reason his touch feels ... not terrible. My hormones would have to agree.

"Yeah, I know we're almost there," I say, opening my eyes and looking up. "But I have to get on another elevator and go even higher."

"Ah," he says, nodding his head slowly, rhythmically. He removes his hand from my shoulder and I oddly wish that he hadn't. "So you're going to the very top."

"I'm only doing this once," I say into his intense and quite gorgeous eyes. "So I might as well do it right."

Like the sound of an angel getting its wings, the elevator dings and comes to a stop. Hail Mary full of grace, I survived. I made it without throwing up or making a complete fool of myself. Well, okay, I made a complete fool of myself, but it could have been far worse. Like plummeting to my death.

The doors open and I make a beeline out of the elevator, ready to push through anyone that gets in my way. Thankfully, the people in the elevator part like the Red Sea and allow me through. I don't make eye contact with anyone as I leave, because I'm pretty sure I know what I'd see there — pity, with a mixture of "she's certifiable." They'd be right; I *am* certifiable. For so many reasons.

Without even a glance out the tall windows, or the people on the observation deck beyond those windows, I walk to the next elevator and get in line. This line is fairly long. Normally I hate long lines like pretty much any other human, but today I don't mind so much. It's giving me a little time to calm down. Although at this point, I think something synthetic would do the job better. Xanax, Klonpin … anesthesia. Luckily, this elevator is a much shorter ride. Google said thirty-six seconds. If it's any longer than that, I will sue Google.

I get behind a rather large man and say a silent prayer that I get to be on a different elevator than him. I'm not being judge-y here. I just really don't want to be in an elevator that is anywhere near the weight capacity. Now that I'm in line and can't look over the edge to see how far up I've come, I can relax a little. At least I can get my breathing under control.

"Did you know the Empire State Building is the fifth tallest building in America?" says a voice coming from a continuous-loop video playing on a screen across from me.

Oh gosh, I think I might be sick again. Why am I even doing this? Right. For Elena. Elena, who would never get to come to the top of this New York City landmark. Elena, who never got to do so many things. I swear, the bucket list she made for me was mostly to mock me from her perch on her heavenly cloud (that's how I like to picture her, at least). It was probably her plan all along. She was clever like that.

But a promise is a promise. And I may be a lot of things, but I'm not a promise breaker. Acrophobic, claustrophobic, agoraphobic, yes. Promise-breaker, no.

"Don't forget the list," Elena had said to me through haggard breathing and closed eyelids.

"I won't," I said, giving her hand a little squeeze, sniffling through tears that wanted to come out, but that I was trying desperately to keep in. I needed to be strong for her.

The list was a bunch of things that Elena always wanted to do, but couldn't. And a bunch of things that I could do, but would never chose to. Like bunging jumping. I tried not to think about all that as I sat next to her, her life slipping away.

"Liza," she had said, opening her eyes wider than I had seen them in a while.

"Yes?" I asked, leaning in so I could hear her. She was so quiet, so fragile.

"Take a chance on ... chance."

Those were her last words to me. *Take a chance on chance.* I've thought of those words during this past year since she's been gone, and I can't figure out what she was trying to tell me. Maybe she meant "take a chance on life," which makes so much more sense. Since she was dying, it may have just been random words that I probably shouldn't read into. Or she could have said it on purpose, knowing I'd dwell on it all the rest of my days, trying to figure out her cryptic message. That would be *so* Elena.

"So you're an Empire State Building virgin," a male voice says behind me, and I jump like a cat that's just seen a cucumber.

"Sorry!" dreamy brown-eyed guy says, his hands up, palms out, as I turn around. "I shouldn't have snuck up on you like that."

My hands go to my chest like my grandmother does when I've just cursed in front of her. *Oh Liza, is that how a lady talks?* she would say. I haven't dared tell her that in New York, I'm considered a lightweight in the cussing department.

"Shoot, I'm really sorry," brown-eyed guy says.

Shoot? This man is *so* not from around here.

"Don't worry about it," I say, and start to turn back around. I really don't want to chitchat. Although staring into his chocolate eyes does sound appealing. But I think I've done enough ogling for one day.

"Is this your first time in the city?" he asks, clearly not reading my body language. Of course, I was doing a half not-wanting-to-talk, half wanting-to-stare-into-his-eyes thing, so who knows what vibe I was giving off.

"Uh, not my first time, no," I say, turning back around to face him.

"But it's your first time in the Empire State Building."

"Yes." I say, keeping my answers simple. Simple is good.

"It's my first time," he says, his hands moving to the pockets of his shorts as he rocks from ball to heel on his feet. "First time in the city and in this building."

I just nod my head, not saying anything. Like an idiot. My hormones, who had started chit-chatting as soon as brown-eyed guy made a reappearance, sigh with disappointment.

"Don't you want to look over the side on this floor before going up?" He asks with a head nod toward the observation deck.

"Nope," I shake my head. "I'm thinking I can only survive one look over the edge, so I'm just going to the top. Don't you want to?"

Would you look there? I'm actually conversing.

"I don't want to ruin the surprise by looking over yet," he says. "Besides, I can catch it on the way down, right?"

"Sure," I say with a dip of my chin. I'll be happily on the ground by then and this whole thing will be over.

In my peripheral vision I catch people moving up in the line, so I turn around and take a few steps to catch up. Every step gets me closer —closer to checking off something on Elena's bucket list. I can't believe it's taken me this long to do anything on the list. A terrible bucket-list-fulfiller, that's what I am. She should've asked someone else. Only there wasn't anyone else to ask. My parents are both scared of everything like me.

"So how many times have you been to the city?" brown-eyed guy asks from behind me. I guess he's not giving up on me. I'm honestly surprised I haven't scared him away yet.

"I don't really know," I say as I turn to face him. "Quite a few times. I grew up about three hours from here."

"Really?" he asks, giving me a once over as if he doesn't believe me. Maybe I don't look like a New York native today, with my cut-off jean shorts, T-shirt, converse, and cross-body black bag over my left shoulder. My goal was comfort. Comfortable enough to run away from this building as fast as I could, if I somehow talked myself out of going up. No such luck.

"Yep," I say. "Born and raised."

"A native New Yorker," he bobs his head toward me, a small smile perched on his lips. Some of his straight, brown hair falls into his eyes and he pushes it back with his hand. His hair is dark. Darker than mine … darker than Elena's.

"So what made you come today, if you hate heights so much?" he asks as we move forward in the line, walking next to each other.

"Just trying something new," I say simply.

He looks at me for longer than a few seconds, as if to read between the lines of what I'm saying. Not like he could know any of it, though. The promise, the bucket list, Elena. Unless he's a mind reader, in which case, I hope he's enjoying the view into the brain of a crazy person that he's getting right now. I'm what Elena always called "a special kind of special." Which is pretty accurate, really.

"I can respect that," he finally says.

"So what brings you here?" I ask, now wanting to keep up the conversation because it's helping pass the time, and also keeping me from thinking of the task at hand (elevator and subsequent looking down from a zillion feet in the sky). He's also a rather nice view, if I'm being honest.

"I'm here on a layover on my way to London,"

he says. "I only have a day."

"Work or play?"

"Both, actually."

"You're by yourself?"

"Yep," he says. "Just me."

We move up in the line, closer to the elevators. With the doors in my line of vision, I'm starting to feel my heart rate pick up again, and the room is suddenly a fifty degrees warmer. Why did Elena want me to go all the way to the top? If I just stayed on this floor—the 86th floor—I could've looked over the side by now and have been down the elevator and on solid ground. Surely that would count? I'm already in line, though. I might as well just get this over with.

"I'm Jay," he says holding out his hand to shake mine.

"Liza," I say, but don't offer him my hand. "My hands are a little sweaty; I'm not sure you want to shake them."

His lips pull up into a half smile, his hand still out. "I'll take my chances."

"Okay, but don't say I didn't warn you," I say, giving him my hand.

His hand feels warm in mine and his handshake is strong, with genuine feeling—none of those dead-fish handshakes here. And there go my hormones again. My already racing pulse picks up a couple of beats.

"Oh yeah, you're right. Gross," he says, taking his hand away from mine, his face contorting into something resembling disgust. He wipes the hand that was holding mine on his shorts.

"Sorry!" I say, wiping both my hands on my jean

shorts, feeling utterly repulsive. "I did warn you."

"Kidding," he says, a smile spreads across his face.

"Wow, you're kind of a jerk, aren't you," I retort, trying to suppress a smile, unsuccessfully.

The line moves up and my smile dissipates. We're getting closer.

Jay clears his throat and my eyes dart away from the elevators and back to his face. Yes, I should focus on that face.

"So did you hear about the restaurant on the moon?" he asks, his face taking on a more serious expression.

"Huh?" I ask, my eyebrows furrowing.

"Great food, no atmosphere." He gives me a little wink.

My chin drops. "Wow, that was bad," I say.

"Why couldn't the bicycle stand up by itself?" He continues, unfazed.

I've heard this one before.

"It was two-tired," he says before I can recall the answer.

"Oh my gosh, you are *not* telling me dad jokes." I glower at him.

He laughs, his head tipping back as he does. He's got one of those contagious laughs. Under different circumstances I would probably join him. Not because of the jokes, mind you.

"How do you tell if a joke is a dad joke?" he asks.

"Because it's super cheesy?"

"No, because it's apparent."

"Oh, gosh, I walked right into that one."

"You really did," he says. "I could tell you

more."

"Please don't," I say, my lips moving to smile without even consulting with me first. Traitorous lips.

"Next!" A woman yells, and I look up to see that we've made it to the front of the line.

"You ready?" Jay asks, motioning with his hand for me to look at the opened elevator waiting for us.

"How—"

"Next!" The woman yells again.

"Shall we?" He puts his hand on the small of my back and guides me through the elevator doors. I hadn't even realized that we'd moved up in the line; he'd kept me occupied with his dumb jokes.

"Thank you," I say as we enter the elevator.

"You're welcome," he says, and then, noticing that his hand is still on my back, he removes it. The spot feels instantly cold. He's crossed so many of my personal lines as a stranger, and yet what bothers me is that it doesn't bother me. I'm kind of a disaster in my head—for so many reasons.

A man in a red vest enters the elevator after about ten of us have filed in, and once the elevator doors close, he slides a metal grate across.

"What the—," I mutter under my breath.

"This elevator has an attendant," Jay half-whispers to me. "I read about it online."

"Why are they double locking us in this box?" I ask, wondering if they have to take extra precautions because we're going so high up. I really wish I could turn back now. Would it be awkward to scream until they opened the doors and let me out? Probably.

"Okay, next stop is floor one-oh-two," the attendant says, like he's done this a million times.

Actually, he probably has. "Over to your left," he points to the left of the doors, "shows how many feet up we'll be. One thousand, two hundred and fifty feet."

My gulp is audible. I know, because most eyes in the elevator turn toward me.

The attendant starts telling us more about the elevator and something about meters. I can't even concentrate. The world around me — well, the box — feels like it's spinning.

"What's the best thing about elevator jokes?" Jay leans down and whispers in my ear.

I'm basically holding my breath at this point so I can't say anything. I just shake my head.

"They work on so many levels."

No words will come out of my mouth.

"That one was the worst, right?"

I look up at him and he's smiling. I nod my head.

"So bad," I'm able to squeak out, my voice so high I sound a little like a dog toy.

And just like that, the elevator dings. I'm not sure how Jay did it, but I survived the ride without a complete breakdown. It took exactly thirty-six seconds (I timed it on my phone). It might have been hard to have a complete breakdown in that time, but I wouldn't put it past me.

Maybe I should offer to buy him coffee after this. Or ask him to father my children because clearly, he gets me. Well, at least the acrophobic part of me. I'm not sure I'm daring enough to ask though. One daring thing at a time.

The attendant pulls open the grate and the doors to the elevator open. Unlike last time, when I made sure I was the first one off, I find that it's not so easy to leave this time. This is it. I'm at the top of a tall building — the fifth tallest in the United State. Oh gosh.

With much trepidation, I take a step outside of the elevator, Jay right behind me. Once outside of the elevator, I see that this floor is much smaller than the 86th. Like, we're basically right here. All I have to do is walk over to those big windows and look down. That's it.

Jay puts his hand on my back again to help guide me, but I'm rooted to this floor. I can't take a step. My heart is pumping and I feel too hot and too cold at the same time. Like I'm freezing, but I'm also sweating. I feel dizzy and my hands are clammy. But most of all, I feel drained. It's like all of my energy was put into getting here and now that I am, I don't know if I can do anymore. I don't know if I can walk the five feet to the window from where I'm planted.

"Hey," Jay says, moving to stand in front of me. "What's going on?"

I don't say anything. I don't move. I'm stuck.

I can't do this.

"What do you think will happen if you look over?" Jay asks, putting a hand on my arm so he can guide me out of the way of the elevator doors I was unknowingly blocking. I slowly move to the wall next to the lift we were in and lean up against it, willing myself to not hyperventilate. Or hurl. Or both.

I take a couple of slow breaths in and out before I answer. "That I'll fall."

"But there are windows," he says.

"I didn't say it was rational," I snap.

"Right," he says, putting a hand through his hair.

"I don't think I can do this," I say, feeling tears form in the corners of my eyes. Oh yes, perfect. Let's add crybaby to my list. Just perfect.

Jay rubs the back of his neck with his hand. I can see him trying to come up with something to say — some words to convince me. But I know me and I won't be convinced.

A tear escapes and travels down the length of my face and down my neck. Another follows. I really hate crying. But I've failed Elena. I broke a promise. And if I can't do this one task — the easiest one on her list — how will I ever do the other ones? I might as well give up now.

"I'm going back down," I say, forcing my eyes to the floor, hoping Jay hasn't seen the tears. "It was nice meeting you," I say to his calves. He really does have nice calves. All manly and muscular looking. I would love one more glance into his eyes, but I don't dare.

I move slowly from the wall and over to the elevator we just got off. The doors open and people trickle out. I look to the attendant and he takes a look at my tear-streaked face and gives me a sympathetic smile. With a hand, he ushers me into the lift. I'm guessing he's seen this before.

I move to the corner of the space, once again gripping the railing. This time though, I'm not as scared of the elevator. Maybe going down isn't as unnerving as going up. Or maybe my shame is masking everything else.

Other people get on the elevator with me. Good things it's elevator etiquette for people to turn around and face the door so they can't see the tears that are flowing down my face rather rapidly now.

The doors start to shut, but then suddenly open back up.

"Can I help you?" The attendant asks.

"I need to get on here," Jay says, his voice intense. My eyes shoot up to catch an eye roll from the attendant and then I see Jay worming his way into the nearly full-to-capacity elevator.

The attendant doesn't look thrilled, but doesn't fight him either.

"What are you doing?" I ask as he joins me in the back corner.

"I'm going back down with you," he says.

"But ... don't you want to look over?" I ask, totally confused.

"I did."

"For a millisecond?"

"It was enough."

"Jay," I say his name like my mom would say mine when she knew I was lying.

"Look," he says, his eyes on mine. "I saw the city; it was a city, and now I'm going back down. Besides, I'm pretty sure you owe me coffee for getting you up here at all."

"I do?"

"Yep. It's the polite thing to do."

I let out a long breath. On the one hand, I could just go home and rest my shame-filled heart. I failed; I should bask in my failure. On the other hand, coffee with a stranger is definitely out of my comfort zone and I'd actually be taking a chance like Elena wanted me to. Yet, on the other hand (I have three hands in this scenario), what if behind those amazing chocolate eyes lays the heart of a serial killer? He doesn't really seem the type, but that's the thing about serial killers.

"Okay," I say. "But only if you're not a serial killer."

"I am," he replies. "But only on Tuesdays."

Despite everything, I smile. "Thank goodness it's Saturday."

CHAPTER 2

"I want to help you," Jay says from across the table at a café that we stopped in to get coffee. I also grabbed myself a small pastry because, in times of need, I've always found sugar to be my best comforter.

"Help me?" I question. "With what?"

"With your fear of heights," he says.

"Are you a professional?" I ask. Good hell, that would totally be my luck to run into a shrink at the Empire State Building. Although who am I to complain about free mental health care, if that's what he's offering. Unless he's planning on charging me, which would be kind of weird ... but, I still might consider it.

"Well, no. I'm an IT consultant, actually," he says.

So not a therapist, then. Is it sad that I'm a little disappointed? I could use some brain-picking right now.

"Thanks, Jay, but there's really no help for me," I say and then take a sip of the hot coffee, feeling it's warmth as it moves down my throat.

"Not according to Google," he says with a quick lift of his brow.

"Google doesn't have a degree in psychology," I say. "And I think that's what I need here."

He chuckles at that. "But people that post on Google have degrees. Or they could be a bunch of posers."

"Posers. That's a good way to describe the internet."

"Regardless, I have a plan," he says with a twinkle in his eye. Or maybe that's mischief. I wouldn't know since I've only known Jay for like an hour.

"I don't know," I say, and then chew on the insides of my cheeks. A habit I had been trying desperately to quit. "Aren't you here to see the sights? Do the tourist thing and all that? You only have one day. Why would you want to spend it trying to help me with my fear of heights?"

"I just do," he says. "Anyway, I do have a list of things I want to see today. Touristy stuff. We can combine it. I promise no dark alleys," he says, holding up his hands, palms facing me.

"I think you might be crazy," I say, picking at a corner of my pastry.

"Maybe. But here's how I see it. I'm all alone visiting a big city by myself, and you," he gestures to me with is hand, "you look like you could be a good tour guide. Plus, I have so many more cheesy jokes I could tell you along the way."

"You have more?"

"Loads of them," he says, the overhead lights sparkling in his chocolate eyes.

I eye him through squinty eyes. I don't know this guy. At all. Even having coffee with him right now is so not me that I'm starting to wonder if the altitude from the Empire State Building did something to my brain. But I also feel an odd connection to him. Like I've met him before. I did just spend a very traumatic moment of my life with him. I wonder if experiencing trauma with someone brings you together.

"I don't know," I say again.

"How about in the name of taking chances?" Jay says, obviously seeing my thought-process playing out on my face.

Take a chance on chance. Elena's words immediately run through my mind. Now why would he even say that? Is her ghost here? Elena promised to haunt me after she died, but I didn't really think she meant it.

"What's your last name?" I ask, still mulling this "plan" over in my head and also keeping an eye out for a possible ghost citing.

"Sanders. What's yours?"

"Parker."

"Liza Parker," he says and then reaches a hand across the table. "Nice to meet you, officially."

"Jay Sanders," I say as I grab a hold of his hand and shake it—this time my hand is not so sweaty. "It's nice to officially meet you as well."

"So, Liza Parker, what's your elevator pitch?" he asks and I cough on the drink I just took. "Sorry, bad choice of words. Tell me about yourself in thirty seconds. You know, like what you would say to someone if you only had an elevator ride to tell them about yourself."

"As opposed to totally freaking out?"

"Well, I did learn a lot about you," he says, a small smirk on his face.

"Yes, all good things," I say, oozing sarcasm.

"You're definitely cute when you're freaking out," he says, grinning.

I feel myself blush instantly. "Well, at least I

have that going for me," I quip.

He studies my face with his eyes, smiling. "So give me your real pitch, then," he says.

"Uh," I say, looking around the room. I don't think I've ever had to explain myself in thirty-seconds. Of course, I've never gone to the top of a building, met a stranger on an elevator, and then had coffee with said stranger. So there are a lot of firsts for me today.

"Do you want me to go first?" he asks.

I motion with my hand, giving him the go-ahead.

"Okay, here goes," he rubs his hands together. "Jay Sanders — which we've already established — I'm from Riverside, California —"

"California?" I cut him off. I would not have pegged him for a Californian.

He gives me a stern but mostly joking look. At least I think he's joking. "The point of an elevator pitch is that there are no interruptions."

"Right. Sorry. Go on." I motion with my hand again.

"Okay, so Jay Sanders, from Riverside, California. I'm twenty-seven and I come from one of those blended California-style families that are all the rage right now. Six siblings, two sets of parents. I own my own IT consulting firm, which has just started to take off and is the reason I'm traveling this weekend. For fun I like the odd comic book, and you can still sometimes find me on my skateboard — I do some of my best thinking there," he adds as an aside. "I don't particularly like talking about politics or religion, even though I have thoughts and beliefs in both. If another guy asks me my favorite movie, I'll tell him it's *Star Wars*, which I do like, but my honest favorite is *Mean Girls*."

"*Mean Girls*? Really?" I scrunch my face. "Like with Lindsay Lohan? Oh, sorry," I say realizing I just interrupted him again. Of course, how could I not. *Mean Girls?*

"Yes," he says with a half-smile, "*Mean Girls.* I don't admit that often. You should feel privileged."

"I'm not sure you should admit it at all," I say.

He laughs a nice hearty laugh. One that makes his fantastic smile seem to reach beyond his eyes.

"You're funny," he says and I blush again. Dang it. "Okay, now you go." He gestures a hand toward me.

"Um, okay," I say feeling uneasiness quiver in my stomach. "I'm Liza Parker—actually Eliza, but only my mom calls me that, and only when she's mad at me. I'm twenty-four and I have one sister and two parents. I'm temporarily working at a paper mill where my dad is floor manager, while I look for a job that I actually like." He chuckles at that. "For fun I like to read books."

Wow, my pitch was totally boring. And short. I've led the most pathetic, boring life thus far. I couldn't even add to my list that I'd been to the top of the Empire State Building and looked over. Which most would consider a pretty uneventful thing. Pathetic.

"You forgot to say where you live," Jay says.

"I already told you where I live. Three hours north of here," I say.

"Yes, but you never said what city."

"Glens Falls. Have you heard of it?"

"No," he says.

"That's why I didn't say the name of my town. No one ever has."

He studies my face. Those eyes have the strangest effect on me.

"Okay so now that we know each other better, what do you think about my plan?" he asks, tapping his finger on the table, anticipating my answer.

"I don't know," I say once more. "I mean, how do we know it'll even work?"

"We don't. It's all about taking chances, and just … seeing." There he goes with the taking chances thing. Elena would probably really like Jay since they seem to have the same line of thinking, especially when it comes to me. Of course, Elena had years to know my neurosis. Jay is only newly privy to my brand of crazy.

"Come on, Liza," he chides.

"Well, you did promise that you weren't a serial killer," I say.

Jay smiles at me like he knows I'm going to say yes to his silly idea.

I roll my eyes, and shake my head, my lips curling up into a small smile. "Okay," I say, not believing any of this is happening.

But I'm stepping out of my comfort zone, right? I probably won't be able to add "spent the day in the city with a complete stranger" to my list, but baby steps. First this, then maybe next I'll be bungee jumping. I seriously doubt that. But who knows. At least I'm taking chances. That's got to count for something.

Plus, I like Jay, despite not really knowing him. There's something about him that I find interesting, not just his good looks. Also, on the off chance he is some sort of psycho, I do have a brand new can of pepper spray in my purse.

"Great," Jay says, smiling and rubbing his hands together again. "Just give me a minute to figure out how we should do this."

Jay goes to work on his phone, typing with his thumbs.

"Okay, I think I've got it," he says after about ten minutes of him typing and me sitting here trying not to freak out. There were a couple of moments that I almost made a run for it, or at least thought about excusing myself to the bathroom and never coming back. But I couldn't do it. Something is keeping me here with him. Maybe it's my interest in what Jay has planned. Yeah, that's what it is. Definitely that. Not some stupid straight-out-of-a-romantic-movie notion that my hormones are cooking up. Stupid hormones.

Jay stands up from the chair he's sitting on and I follow suit. But instead of going to leave like I thought we were, he pulls the chair I was sitting on next to his. With one swift movement, he stands on the chair. He offers a hand to me to help me up on the chair next to him.

"What are you doing?" I ask, looking around at the people in the café who are now focusing on Jay.

"We're starting small," he says.

"Jay," I say looking up at the ridiculousness in front of me. "I'm not scared of standing on a chair."

"Prove it," he says, hand still out.

"This is embarrassing," I say, still not giving him my hand.

"Come on," he thrusts his hand out farther.

I roll my eyes and give him my hand. He helps pull me up to the chair next to him and now we're standing next to each other on chairs in the middle of a café. This is utterly ridiculous.

"How does it feel?" Jay asks, letting go of my hand and taking in the view of the café.

"It feels ridiculous," I say.

"But you're not scared?"

"Not even in the slightest," I say. "But then again, if I fall, I'm pretty sure I won't die. I doubt I'd even break anything."

"Good point," he says, jumping off his chair and giving me a hand to help me down from mine.

"You've passed the first height with flying colors," he says, his chocolate eyes dancing with excitement. "What do you think?"

"I think you're mental," I say with a chuckle.

"No way. Stick with me, Liza." He smiles brightly.

My hand still in his, he pulls me and my reluctant body out of the café.

~*~

"Okay, look over," Jay says as we stand on a bridge in Central Park.

It should feel weird standing here with Jay on this beautiful cobblestone bridge covered with bright green vines, the mid-morning light shining through the trees and sparkling on the water below. But it doesn't. It feels strangely good. And this coming from someone who just had what was most likely a nervous breakdown not that long ago. Of course, that could mean there's some brain fog going on. But whatever it is, I feel safe. Which is totally not normal—maybe I should have my head examined for real.

"Look," he says, motioning toward the edge.

I scrunch my face at him and then turn and take the two steps to get to the edge. I look over.

"So, how're you feeling?" he asks. He moves to stand next to me, his face turned toward me. So close that I can feel his breath on my neck. That's actually more unnerving than the edge I'm looking over right now.

I clear my throat in an attempt to ground myself. "Well, let's see," I say. "We're about twelve feet up, from what I can guess." I motion toward the water. "The height doesn't bother me as much as the water below does. I mean, if I fell from here, chances are I would survive. But, like, what kind of germs are floating in that water?"

"Oh hell, you're a germaphobe too?" he asks, his face full of humor.

"No!" I say quickly. "I'm not a germaphobe. That water just looks gross ... like, kinda germy."

"So being bothered by germs doesn't make you a germaphobe."

"No, I just don't—. Okay, fine. I'm a bit of a germaphobe," I say, feeling heat crawl up my face.

"Come on phobia girl," he says, his hand on the small of my back again as he guides me off the bridge. "We've got more to see."

As we walk through Central Park, I feel ... good. Relaxed even. I'm on solid ground, and it's a beautiful day. Plus, it's been a while since I just walked through Central Park, taking in the scene around me, breathing in the scent of fresh cut grass that seems to be coming from everywhere. Walking with Jay right now, I think I'm seeing it through a new pair of eyes. I don't think I've ever done anything in Manhattan with a first-timer. I love seeing how his eyes light up as he takes it all in. The lush green trees and grass, the beautiful park benches that line each side of the path we're on. The bum sleeping on one of them.

I guess it can't all be perfect.

"Tell me about Glens Falls," Jay says as we walk.

"There's not much to tell," I say with a shrug. "It's a small town. Used to be a mill town, but it's pretty depressed right now. It's on the way from Albany to Lake Placid, at the foot of Lake George and the Adirondacks. I actually didn't grow up there. Up until I was thirteen we lived in Corinth, which is an even smaller town. Actually, it's barely a town. More like a spec in the middle of nowhere."

"Why did you move?"

Because my sister was sick. Because the hospital was in Glens Falls and it was safer to live closer, and easier as she got worse. It was all for Elena.

But I don't tell him that. "That's where the paper mill is. It was easier for my dad," is all I say.

"So California," I say, moving the question back to him.

"Yep," he says. "Born and raised."

"I wouldn't have pegged you for California."

"Really? Why's that?" he asks, looking a little insulted.

"Aren't most Californians blonde and blue-eyed? And everyone talks like a surfer?"

"As opposed to everyone from New York having dark hair and dark eyes and talking like *The Godfather*?"

"Right," I say through a laugh. I've got dark hair, but my eyes are blue. And I definitely don't talk like someone from *The Godfather*. At least I don't think I do.

The conversation flows easily between us as we walk. We talk about how we got into the work we do. Jay went to school for information technologies, and got a job right out of college. He soon found that he hated working for other people, so he started his own thing with the help of his stepsister who can "sell anything to anyone." I actually think Jay's a pretty decent salesman himself. He convinced me to spend the day with him, after all. I'm still not entirely sure how that happened. But with each passing minute, I'm happy I did.

Jay has a contagious energy. It makes me wish I was more like him. More daring, more interesting. I've become sort of a hermit lately. I think need to change that.

"Are you ready for the next stop?" he asks as we leave the quiet embrace of the park for a busy Manhattan street.

"Sure," I say, even though I'm not ready to leave the park. Talking with Jay, experiencing all of this through his eyes, I don't know if the next stop will have the same feeling or dynamic. Plus, I'm slightly scared of what he might put me through next.

"Let's go."

CHAPTER 3

"I would not have pegged you for a lover of modern art," I say as we stand outside the doors of the Museum of Modern Art. It's been about a decade since I last stood at these doors. The last time I was here was when I was in high school for my sophomore class trip.

He pauses, his hand on the handle of the entrance, his brow furrowed. "What kinds of things *did* you peg me for?" Some of his bangs fall in his face as he talks, and he pushes them back with his fingers.

"Hmm," I say putting a finger to my chin as I ponder. "A serial killer?"

"Only on Tuesdays," he quips as he opens the door and a blast of cold air-conditioning hits my face.

We get in back of the line, which isn't that long for this time of year and day. It only takes a few minutes in line before Jay purchases us tickets (even though I throw a tantrum because he paid for mine without asking) and we enter the main exhibit area. Jay heads toward the elevators and I feel panic race through me. I don't think this building is very tall; however, I'm not really keen on elevators today.

"They have escalators," I say, pointing over to the escalators to the left of us.

"Yes, but this is a short elevator ride. It's good practice," he says, nodding toward the pewter colored doors just ahead of us.

I blow air out of my lips and let my shoulders sag. My poor attempt at a pout. I doubt it was even remotely cute, but I wasn't really going for that.

"We're just going to the fifth floor," he says as we take the few steps needed to arrive at our destination.

I swallow loudly. "Just the fifth floor?"

"Yes, I promise," he says, a soft smile on his lips as he presses the up arrow on the elevator.

We enter the elevator and I breathe deeply. Normally I wouldn't even care about a five-floor climb in an elevator. But today, I care. Maybe I have PTSD.

"Why do bees hum?" Jay asks as the elevator starts to move up.

"Oh gosh, please, not more dad jokes," I say with a roll of my eyes, but a small smile on my face. My dad offers crappy jokes and puns all the time and it used to drive Elena and me insane. For some reason, they aren't so bad coming from Jay. Don't get me wrong, they're totally not funny, but I just can't bring myself to mind. Also, it's kind of cute.

"Humor me," he says.

"Okay, why do bees hum?" I ask, my voice flat, keeping up the pretense. He doesn't need to know it doesn't bother me.

"Because they don't know the words," he says with a half-grin and an eyebrow lift.

"Yeah, that was terrible," I say, even though I'm smiling.

"Don't worry, there's more," he says with a smile that I can't help but enjoy. Jay has a spectacular smile. It doesn't just go to his eyes, it's like it goes all the way to the sky. Big and broad, and nice, white teeth. He should be in an advert for toothpaste. They'd sell millions.

The bell rings and the elevator doors open and we walk out, Jay's hand going to the small of my back again, anchoring me. Such an odd familiarity accompanying the gesture, with the familiar feelings becoming even more defined every time he touches me there. Almost like a strong sense of déjà vu or something. This is all so weird. I think I'll just try not to think about it too much.

As we walk out, a sign points to the exhibit, but Jay steers me in a different direction and stops me as we stand near a half-wall railing that overlooks the atrium in this building. I saw a sign for the Marron Atrium when we first entered. I had a feeling I was going to have to look down at it from above.

"Ready?" he asks, not questioning my intelligence by even asking me if I know what his plans are.

"Sure," I say, as I take the teeniest, tiniest steps over to the edge.

As we get closer, Jay puts his hands on my hips, keeping a small gentlemanly distance between us. "I've got you. You won't fall over. Now look."

His hands on my hips would normally seem like a creepy-creeper move, but somehow it doesn't. It feels like he is genuinely trying to make me feel safe. How someone I barely know could make me feel this way is crazier than going to the top of the Empire State Building, honestly. At least, for me it is.

I peer over the ledge of the railing and look down.

"Okay, that's kinda far," I say. "I would definitely die if I fell over."

"But you won't fall over, I have you," he says, still standing behind me, his hands still on my hips.

"Focus on the other things, rather than how far down the floor is," he says leaning in so he's looking over my shoulder.

I'm actually finding it hard to focus on anything but him behind me and the small space between us that just got smaller, to be perfectly honest.

"Um," I say, as I peer over just a tiny bit farther. "I guess I like the way the light makes shadows around the space." The contrast of the light and dark around the room is rather striking.

"Good," he says. "What else do you see?"

His breath is on my neck again, and oh wow, he smells good. Soap and a bit of fresh cut grass. Which would make sense since we were in Central Park not too long ago. With my luck I probably picked up the not-so-lovely smells of the city, like body odor or homeless guy. Suddenly the closeness of him is making me feel rather self-conscious.

"Did I lose you?" Jay asks, nudging me a little to the side so he can see my face, his hands still on my hips holding me steady.

"Sorry," I say, feeling like such a girl right now. I am one, so this isn't too shocking. "It's not quite as scary when I don't focus on how far down everything is."

"Great," he says pulling away from me. "You passed. Can I interest you in some Van Gogh?" he says as I turn around and face him.

"Sounds Van Good," I say, and then cringe at my terrible pun. I can't believe I just went there.

"Ah, young grasshopper, you are learning," Jay says in a terrible Japanese accent.

CHAPTER 4

Please don't stop here. Please don't stop here. Please don't stop here.

"And here we are," Jay says as we stop in front of Rockefeller Center. Obviously I knew we were stopping here, since it's a total touristy place to go, but I still hoped.

"I'm *not* going up there," I say as we stop in front of the seriously tall building. I plant my feet firmly on the sidewalk, my stance immovable. Well, I'm sure it's moveable, as Jay is quite a bit taller and bigger than me. But I can put up a good fight if needs be. Plus, there's always the pepper spray.

Jay shakes his head. "I wasn't going to make you go up there," he points to the top. "I do need to make a call, though. So just hang for a second."

He walks about ten feet away from me, his back toward me. Which leaves me time to stare at his backside without being caught ogling. I have to say, it's a nice backside. My giddy hormones giggle inside my stomach. Down, ladies.

"Okay, thanks so much. I owe you," he says after a very brief phone conversation that I caught bits and pieces of. Because I was eavesdropping, obviously.

He pockets the phone as he walks toward me.

"So if we aren't going to the top, what are we doing?" I ask, really wanting to know what his plan is so I can start preparations for my probable panic attack.

"It's a surprise. I had to call in a favor," he says.

I eye him suspiciously. "What kind of favor?" I ask.

"You'll see."

Five minutes later, guided by an employee of the building and after a short ride up an elevator—which was surprisingly not too bad—Jay and I stand looking over what appears to be a rooftop garden.

"Oh wow," I say as I look around the beautifully manicured space. It's a garden. On a rooftop. In all my life, I've never actually seen one. Probably because I hate rooftops, but wow, I've been missing out. The stark contrast between building top and the bright greenery is almost breathtaking. Or I may have just forgotten to breathe since we're up high and all that.

"Beautiful," Jay says as he takes a step forward, looking around at the sight in front of us.

It's set up like a courtyard with stone planter boxes filled with buxus hedging surrounding the outer edge. More hedging, topiaries, and bright flowers in more stone planter boxes make up the middle area, forming a small courtyard with seating. Near the back end is a square water feature with a golden statue of a frog with water spouting out of its mouth.

"I've never seen anything like it," I say.

"Me either," Jay says. "I mean, I saw it online when I was planning my day here, but in person, it's even more amazing."

"Why are we practically the only people up here?" I ask, spying a few people in the corner having a chat. They look more like they work here in their business attire. Definitely not tourists.

"Because it's closed to the public," he says.

"How did you get us up here?"

"My stepsister knows the guy that took us up here," he says and then gives me a buoyant smile.

"Nice to have hook-ups," I say, my eyes taking in my surroundings again.

"That's about the only hook-up I have," he says.

"I can get you a tour of a paper mill," I say. "Sadly, that's my only hook-up."

"A paper mill, you say?" Jay puts an index finger to his chin, deliberately trying to look pensive. "Sounds fascinating."

"Oh, it really is," I say, oozing sarcasm. "You'll love the smell."

"I'll add it to my bucket list," he says, not carrying the sarcasm in his tone that I would've expected. Maybe he's serious?

He motions to a bench and we sit down. The buildings near us seem so close, like I could reach out and touch them. And it's quiet up here. So quiet.

Jay and I sit in companionable silence, both of us taking in our surroundings. He's so close, his leg is touching mine just barely. I try not to concentrate on it too hard so that my hormones don't up and make some sort of cheerleading pyramid. But the not-concentrating only takes my mind to that other place—the one that I've tucked in the corner, but I can still barely hear screaming "*Who are you and what have you done with Liza!*" The part of my brain that keeps me safe from doing crazy things like this. Sitting on a rooftop garden with someone who was a complete stranger not even hours ago. And for all intents and purposes, is still a stranger. On paper, at least he is. Off paper, he seems like someone I've known for ages. I've read about this kind of phenomenon in books and heard others speak of it, but it's never actually happened to me.

I decide to just focus on what's around me rather than the war going on inside my head.

"Elena would love this," I say out loud without thinking.

"Elena?" Jay asks.

Oh man, I so hate my mouth right now.

"My sister," I say, after trying to figure out what I could say, but then settling on the truth.

He just nods and doesn't ask follow-up questions. Crisis averted.

"Come on," he says standing up, and I follow suit. "Time to look over the edge."

"Do we have too?" I say, refusing to move, even when I feel the pressure of his hand on my back as he tries to guide me over to the side. I don't want to ruin this magical place by looking over the stupid edge and realizing we aren't in our own oasis, but rather eleven stories off the ground.

"Come on, Liza," he says. "You can do it."

I let out a long exhale. Jay moves his hand from my back and grabs my hand in his. My stomach does a somersault and my hormones sigh in unison. His hand feels soft but manly at the same time. And quite large compared to my hand. I feel all feminine and girly.

He pulls me just slightly and I acquiesce with only little resistance. He walks me to the space in between two of the stone planter boxes and stands next to the cement railing that comes up to about mid-waist. He looks over, my hand still in his.

"Have a look," he says after looking over. "It's not that scary."

"Easy for you to say," I say and give him pouty lips. "You're not scared of heights."

"Or germs," he adds with a half-smile.

And other things, I think to myself. I'm glad I didn't let it all hang out in the beginning so he would know what a freak I really am. Better to not let your freak-flag wave too high. Or maybe it's better to put it all out there so they know what they're getting into from the get-go. Too late for that now, I guess.

I inch closer to the ledge and peek over the top. Below us is a street. I can't even orient myself to figure out what street it is. I'm pretty sure it's 5th Avenue, but I've never been any good at directions — right, left, north, south — none of it. I can see quite a few people walking around looking at shops. Groups of tourists together, couples holding hands, small gatherings of people — maybe family, maybe friends — out for a drink. If I focus on that, it's not so bad. If I focus on the fact that if Jay pushes me over right now, I would pretty much go splat all over the ground, that's when I feel a throbbing sensation in my head as my heart-rate picks up speed, making my face flush and red-hot heat spread through my limbs.

"You're safe," Jay says to me. He lets go of my hand and hooks his hand around my waist and pulls me into him. I take in a shaky breath. *I am safe. I am safe.*

I. Am. Safe.

Nope. I'm not convincing myself. I better go back to looking around what's below me rather than picturing my body splattered on the floor below.

Which is just the loveliest picture. I really and truly need therapy.

"Look over there," Jay says, pointing down and to my right. My eyes follow where he's pointing and I see street performers dancing to music I can barely hear.

"And there," he points farther down the street and my eyes follow his hand until I see what he's pointing at. A crowd exiting St. Patrick's Cathedral, probably leaving after mass.

Jay's arm around my waist, focusing on other things from this view, my heart slows just the slightest bit. But it's enough. We stand in silence, his arm still around me, our bodies close together. Of course, now that I just focused on the closeness of his proximity, my heart starts to pick up again.

"So what do you think?" he asks quietly, turning his head toward me.

"I think it's not so bad," I say. I turn my face toward him, not realizing how close he is.

Our eyes lock, and it's as if everything around us — the hustle and bustle of the street below — has all paused. The only thing I can hear is our intertwining breath. My stomach does a little twirl and it feels like the whole world goes silent as his eyes travel down my face and to my lips. He leans in toward me. Only centimeters between us now. I can feel his breath on my lips and my heart races with the thrill of it. The thumping of my heart is drowning out the warning bells that are going off in my head.

A throat clears behind us and we both jump, Jay's arm unhitching from my side, and without his grip keeping me upright, I fall right into a hedge.

"Time's up," says the employee that brought us

up here.

Jay works to pull me from the bush, and I can't help but start laughing at the absurdity of it all. Jay and me, almost lip-locking it up on a rooftop garden. Of course, it was rather romantic and all that. But seriously, what is going on with my brain? I don't know Jay. Not that well, at least. I don't kiss strangers. I wouldn't even do seven minutes in heaven with Richie Staley at a party in the eighth grade because, you know, germs. And I've known Richie my entire life. This whole thing is so not me.

"You okay?" Jay asks as he finally rights me, a smile on his face. I try to stifle my giggling, but then it comes out as a snort and sets us both laughing. Employee guy is not happy.

"Sorry," Jay says to the man. He puts his hand on my back and we follow our not-amused guide out of the garden.

CHAPTER 5

"Holy crap," I say as we arrive at our next stop.

"The High Line is what it's called," Jay says, hands on his hips as he takes it all in. "A friend of mine told me about it."

We walked five blocks from Rockefeller Center, grabbing something to eat from a street vendor along the way, which was much needed as my stomach was actually growling.

"It's amazing," I say, turning around in my spot for a three-sixty view.

We're standing in a park built on an old freight rail line and we're above — *above* — the busy streets of Manhattan. I focus on the beauty around us and try not to think about the fact that if there was an earthquake, we would be first to go down (I hate my brain). We're at the beginning of a walkway that I can't even see the end of, with tall wild grass and various flowerbeds dotting the sides. Views of the Hudson River to our right, and artwork of all kinds popping up here and there. It's seriously amazing. I mean, who thinks to build a park on an old rail line? New Yorkers, that's who.

"Come on," Jay says, as he sees a series of steps where you can sit and look through a window of the busy street below. "Let's sit."

I don't know if Jay's therapy — or whatever it is he's doing — is working, but the height right now isn't bothering me so much. Well except for my initial worry that we might collapse in an earthquake, which I don't know has *ever* even happened in the history of this city. Also, we really aren't that high up, so maybe that's helping as well.

Jay doesn't sit as close to me this time, almost as if on purpose. Like we crossed a line on the rooftop and he doesn't want to go there again. Of course, I'm a dumb girl and I read into everything. I internally roll my eyes at myself for even going there, and also for being a dumb girl.

"Tell me something no one knows about you," Jay says after we've sat in silence for a bit, looking at the cars and taxis driving on the road beneath us.

"Something no one knows?" I take my eyes off the street and move them to him, repeating his question because it catches me so off guard.

"Yeah. What secrets does Eliza Parker have?" he asks, turning his head toward me, a smile on his face.

"Wouldn't it be easier if I told you something *you* don't know? I mean, there's quite a bit to tell since we just met this morning," I say.

"Yeah, but I want to know something no one else knows."

"Why?" I ask.

"So I can put it away and save it as a reminder of this day. When I remember my day here, I can think of this girl I met and the secret she told me that no one else is privy to."

"Okay," I say more in the form of a question, and full of skepticism.

"Come on," he says. "What've you got?"

"I don't know," I say, wracking my brain for something no one knows, something I've never told anyone. I don't have to go far, though. There's something I've never told anyone, but I'm not sure I want to go there right now.

He scoots to cover the inches that were separating us and nudges me with his shoulder.

I take a deep breath and will my hormones to simmer down at his proximity.

"Okay," I say, angling my body toward him just slightly. "My sister, Elena—"

"Yeah," he says, interjecting.

"She, um ... she died a year ago."

"Oh," he says, his head pulling back quickly, shock on his face.

I look away from him because I hate seeing sadness in people's eyes, and I know it's coming because that seems to be the only emotion humans can muster when they find out about Elena. Of course, I'm not sure what else they could feel. But I wish it wasn't sadness. I don't want people to feel sad for me.

I chew on the insides of my cheek. "Elena was born with a heart defect and she lived a lot longer than she was supposed to, but," I lick my lips, "it wasn't a great life. Lots of hospital stays and doctors' visits. We couldn't travel or do normal family things because there was always worry about Elena and her heart."

Jay reaches over and takes my hand, lacing his fingers through mine. The comforting gesture makes my eyes well up and I so do *not* want to cry right now. I don't like to cry. I don't like to be serious. Just telling him this is making me feel loads of uncomfortable and I find myself wanting to make a quip or a joke to change the feeling in the air.

"Go on," he says quietly.

"Anyway, so Elena couldn't do much — she had to be careful because of her heart. Her life, as you can imagine, wasn't very daring." I reach for my purse that was hanging by my side and pull it into my lap, unlatching the magnetic button and opening the flap. I slip my hand inside and find the piece of paper I'm looking for and pull it out. "So she made me this list, before she passed, of things she always wanted to do but couldn't. And she asked me to do them for her. I've never told anyone about it."

Jay reaches for the piece of paper, but stops short. "Can I see it?"

I hand it to him and he unlinks his hand from mine, opening the paper.

"That's quite the list," he says after he's read it. He points to the paper, "Did she really think you would go bungee jumping?"

I laugh because I hate the thickness in the air that has landed on our conversation, and also because for as little time as Jay has known me, he actually has me pretty figured out.

"Sometimes I wonder if she made the list to spite me," I say, and then bite the inside of my cheek. "She was pretty hilarious, actually."

"I bet she was," he says, folding the paper up and handing it back to me. I tuck it in my purse.

"So that's why you were attempting the Empire State Building," he says, nodding his head, his face registering the truth.

"Yep," I say. "And also why I felt like I failed when I couldn't do it." I look down at my hands twiddling nervously in my lap.

"Wow, I'm sorry," he says, wholeheartedly. "I feel bad."

"Yeah, most people do when I talk about Elena," I say, my shoulders lifting in a brief shrug.

"No—I mean yes—I'm sorry about your sister, but I feel bad that your secret was so ... uh, deep," he says.

"I thought that was the point," I say, eyeing him suspiciously.

"Well maybe, but my secret that I was going to tell you was that I tell everyone I'm allergic to coconut, but the truth is, I just hate it."

"What?" I slap him on the arm—harder than I mean to. "That's it? That's your secret no one else knows? Who even cares whether you like coconut!"

"My bad," he says, hands up, palms facing toward me, his mouth trying desperately not to break into a smile. I must be giving him my most incredulous look. Because that's how I feel: incredulous and pissed and totally duped. But at the same time, I can feel a giggle bubbling up inside of me. Jay does weird things to me.

"You know," I say slapping him on the arm again for good measure. "I think I've just become a serial killer on Saturdays."

I must have said this loudly because suddenly there are quite of few pairs of eyes on us.

"She's kidding," Jay says to our crowd of onlookers, but then turns to me and under his breath says, "You *are* kidding, right?"

"I wouldn't be so sure," I say, trying to keep the smile that's dying to break across my face from coming out. No such luck.

Jay laughs when he sees me smile, and then grabs my hand and pulls me to standing.

"Come on," he says. "We've got more to see."

After that, the feeling in the air is much lighter. And fun. I like it. It's been so long since I did something fun for myself. We walk along the path, taking in everything around us and talking. He asks a lot of questions about Elena and it feels good to talk about her, almost cathartic.

"So what else besides work do you have planned for London?" I ask as we walk. The tall grass edging the sides of the trail moves softly with the late-afternoon breeze.

"I have to mostly work, but I plan to take a day or two to do other things," he says.

"Touristy things?"

"Well, yes, but I'm also there to help with a foundation I'm involved in," he says.

"A foundation? More information, please."

He chuckles at my demanding tone. "I work with a foundation that supplies hearing aids for children that are born with hearing loss. Their headquarters are in London."

I turn my head to see his face. His eyes are forward and he looks pensive. Or maybe shy. Like this is information he doesn't go telling everyone about.

"Why that particular foundation?" I ask.

"My little brother was born with hearing loss, so it's something I'm passionate about."

"So," I say, tucking my hair behind my ears. "You like to help people."

"Well," he chuckles, "yeah. I do."

"So I'm a charity case, then?" my mouth asks without consulting my brain.

"What?" He turns his face toward mine and his eyes are huge with surprise. "No," he shakes his head slowly. "Actually, I wanted to spend the day with you for purely selfish reasons. The height thing was just an excuse."

"Oh," I say, because I can't seem to find words right now. Plus my hormones are doing some sort of hip-hop dance in my stomach from his words, and I'm finding it hard to speak.

"So, are you ready for our next stop?" Jay asks, as we arrive at the end of the High Line.

"There's more?" I ask, still reeling from his comment and also feeling like he's gone way above and beyond today. The thought of spending more time with him does make me happy though. I'm not ready to be done.

"Yep," he says, taking my hand. "One more stop."

CHAPTER 6

"Of course your hotel is in Times Square. How very touristy of you," I say in mocking tones.

"Well, I *am* a tourist, so..." he trails off as we enter the elevator inside Jay's hotel and he hits the button for the forty-eighth floor.

Floor forty-eight. *I will not freak out. I will not freak out.*

"You're totally freaking out right now, aren't you," Jays says, moving across the empty elevator to stand next to me. Empty, except for us. It's a glass elevator, so I stand against the wall and close my eyes and try not to think of all the ways I might die on this elevator.

"Not freaking out," I say pitifully.

"What do you call cheese that's not yours?"

"Seriously?"

"Nacho cheese," he says with a smile, hip-checking me as he does.

"Terrible," I say, and if my eyes were open, I would totally roll them.

"Why do crabs never give to charity?" he asks and I moan dramatically. "Because they're *so* shellfish."

"Please make it stop," I say.

"The elevator or the jokes?" he asks.

"Both."

The elevator makes a pinging noise and I look up to see that we've made it to our intended destination. His cheesy dad jokes, as terrible as they are, have definitely served a purpose.

"Shall we?" he asks, offering me an arm.

"Sure," I say, wrapping a hand around his arm as he guides me out of the elevator.

He leads me into a lounge-type area and asks for a table by the window. I hold back a *hell no* at his window seat request. I'm going to try wearing some big girl pants and just deal. Because I'm an adult and I can totally do this. Maybe.

We're seated by the window with a beautiful view of the city. Only it takes me a minute to realize that my view is, well, changing.

"What the—"

"I hope you don't get motion sickness," Jay interjects. "It's a revolving floor. We'll get to see the whole city from right here." He pokes the table with is finger.

"No motion sickness," I say, grateful that I don't have yet one more thing *not* going for me. I take a long look out the window. I should be totally freaked out by the height and the view, but we're moving! "Wow," is all I can say.

"Glad you like it," Jay says, sounding quite pleased with himself.

The server comes over and we order appetizers and drinks. The platform we're on moves slowly, and I find myself staring out the window, not wanting to miss a thing. I know we're forty-eight floors above the ground, and I know I'm basically looking over an edge, but for some reason I'm okay with it. Huh. Weird.

"It's amazing," I say, taking in the view with the setting sun splaying beautiful tones of pink and gold

across the sky. It's breathtaking — but in a good way.
Not in a get-me-off-this-crazy-horse kind of way.

Our drinks arrive and we sip as we look out the
window at this view of the city. It's the perfect
setting to the end of the day — a day I don't really
want to end. But I know it will. This is Jay's hotel,
and when we're done here, I'll leave him and either
train it back home, or call my aunt and see if I can
crash on her couch. I feel suddenly sad that it's
nearly over, this day of taking chances. Sure, they
weren't specifically on Elena's list, but everything I
did today was way more than I'd ever dared do
before.

It makes me think that I could maybe try other
things. Not bungee jumping — let's not get crazy. But
maybe instead of looking for a job in Glens Falls, I
could move to the city. I could get a job here, find an
apartment — nothing above the second floor, of
course (baby steps). But I feel like the whole world
has suddenly opened up to me, and I kind of want to
jump in and take advantage of it all.

"What are you thinking about?" Jay asks. I turn
to find his chocolate eyes on me, and I wonder how
long he's been watching me.

I sigh. "I was thinking that maybe I could live
here." I turn and look out the window again, spying
my arch-nemesis in the backdrop. The Empire State
Building. Although, if it wasn't for that ridiculously
tall building, and my crazy neuroses, I wouldn't be
sitting here, looking at this view, with this person
that I feel like I've known for a long time.

"You could totally live here," Jay says
confidently. "You should do it."

Our appetizers arrive just as we're above Times

Square. The bright lights make it seem like the ground is glowing from up here. Lights dance and flash all around us. I think I can appreciate Times Square more from up here; down below it's full of people and taxis with constantly honking horns. I like being encapsulated up here much better.

Even with the slow movement of the floor, the time seems to fly. Before I know it, the waiter brings our bill just as we've made a full three-sixty view of the city. Jay drops a card on the check, clearly saying without words that he's paying. I go to protest, but then figure what's the point? He's won every time today.

I look a little closer at Jay's credit card and see that there's a C in front of his name. *C. Jay Sanders.* Jay has a first name that I don't even know about. It actually makes me smile. For all I know about him, there's still so much I don't know. I can only hope that this isn't the end for Jay and me. I want to keep him in my life, even if it's from across the country.

"So," Jay says, looking at me as if he was just thinking the same thing — that he doesn't want this to be the end. Of course, I could be totally reading him wrong. My hormones seem to want to me to think that way.

"So," I echo him.

"What do you think of my — well, Google's — therapy?" He asks, a small smile on his lips. They really are nice lips. Makes me wish we hadn't been interrupted on that rooftop garden.

"I think it might have worked," I say with a little shrug of my shoulders.

"Why do you think it worked?" Jay asks, his face not looking convinced.

"Jay," I say, putting my hands on the table we're sitting at, "I'm forty-eight floors above the ground, sitting at a table by the window, and I haven't felt one ounce of panic." I give him one of my biggest smiles.

"Except for the elevator ride up here," he says.

"Except for that," I agree.

"Well, then I think we have only one more stop," he says.

"No, Jay," I shake my head. "You've been great. This whole day," I gesture around the room with my hands, "has been great."

"Just one more stop," he says.

"Aren't you tired? Don't you need to get some rest before you travel tomorrow?" I ask. I'm not sure why I'm protesting. Wasn't I just wishing this day wouldn't end? And here he's offering me more time.

"I'm not tired, and who needs rest? I can sleep on the plane," he says. "Come on, Liza. One more stop."

I look to the side as if contemplating, but who am I kidding? "Okay."

He stands up from the table, offering me a hand to get up. "Then let's go."

CHAPTER 7

"You're kidding me, right?" I say as we approach the building that was formerly known as the Empire State Building, but will now be known as my arch nemesis.

"Come on, Liza," he says. "You can totally do this."

"I'm pretty sure I can't," I say, looking up. Oh gosh, his therapy didn't work. At all. The panicky feeling, my heart picking up its pace, the need to hurl up the food we just ate—it's all back, and with a vengeance.

"You *can*," Jay says, putting his hand on my arm. "Don't you want to do this for Elena?"

Of course I want to do it for Elena, I just don't think I can. Marking off something on her stupid list was the reason I came here today. I wrap my arms around my torso, hugging myself tightly and look up again.

Jay moves in closer to me, his face serious. "You can do this, I promise. I'll be with you the entire time."

"I don't know, Jay."

"How about this," he says, his hand going under my chin and lifting my face toward his. "We'll try one more time. If you can't do it, then we'll just get on the elevator and come back down. Okay?"

I close my eyes, feeling like I'm starting at square one.

"No," I say shaking my head.

"No?" he questions.

"If we're going up there, I'm looking over," I say, and then take a deep breath. I can do this. I am strong. I did a lot of things I wouldn't normally do today, and now I want to be able to actually mark something off Elena's list.

Jay's smile reaches the sky again. He grabs my hand and, without a word, pulls me inside the building.

The lines and the ticket purchasing and elevator rides are like a blurred out-of-body experience. When the second elevator reaches the 102nd floor and the attendant opens the door, I slam right back into my body again and feel the ever-present terror of what's ahead of me. My feet once again plant themselves on the floor just outside the elevator.

I can't move. I'm totally going to fail Elena — and myself — again.

"Close your eyes," Jay says, taking my hand in his.

"No way," I protest.

"Just do it — I'll guide you," he says.

I struggle internally for a few seconds, but then I close my eyes and after a bit, my stance slackens and I let Jay guide me.

"Okay, you can open your eyes," he says.

I slowly open my eyes and look. My heart flutters in my chest and my breathing picks up.

"Tell me what you see," Jay says as he moves behind me, putting his hands on my hips like he did before, steadying me.

"I see—" I start, then swallow hard. I see that we're a long way up. But I know that's not what he's asking. "Um, I see lights. Lots of lights." I focus on all the lights twinkling around the city like a million tiny stars.

"Good," he says, moving in closer. My body automatically leans back against him and my hormones do a cheer. But it feels good to lean against Jay. He's been kind of like an anchor since I met him.

"What else do you see?" he asks.

"I see ... everything," I say.

"Everything?"

"I mean, it feels like I can see the entire world from here," I say.

"Liza," Jay says in my ear. "You did it."

I take in a quick breath. *I did it.*

I spin around and put my arms around Jay, and hug him tight, burying my head into his warm chest.

"I did it!" I say, pulling my head back so I can see his face.

In your face, people who didn't believe in me. Which is no one, since only Jay knows I'm doing this.

I look to Jay and his smile has reached the sky again. "Now you can officially cross something off the list."

I touch my purse with the list in it, nodding my head. Elena would be so proud.

Jay keeps his arms around me and moves us so we can both look out the window again. I lay my head on his chest, feeling his warmth and comfort and look out at the city below me.

I pull my head away from his chest and look at his face. "Thank you."

"You're welcome," he says, locking his eyes with mine.

The air between us changes. I feel like I might

need to blink, but I don't want to break the spell I'm suddenly under.

"Liza," Jay whispers my name as his eyes move down to my mouth. His hand moves up to my face and he caresses the side of my jaw with his thumb.

He leans in, and then I lean in, and before some idiot can interrupt us, his lips are on mine. My hormones immediately start in with the hallelujah chorus. His lips are soft and spectacular at the same time. Our mouths meld together almost as if they were meant to do this. Like our lips are matches for each other.

I pull him toward me and he deepens the kiss. I never want this kiss to end. I never want this night to end. I just want to stay up here on the top of the Empire State Building, basking in the glory of overcoming one of my biggest fears, and locking lips with this very amazing man.

After basically making out for a couple of minutes and not carrying one iota about the PDA we're demonstrating right now, Jay slows the kiss and then pulls away, but keeps his face close to mine. My lips feel like they're on fire.

We smile at the same time.

"That was—"

"Totally," I say, cutting him off, knowing exactly what he means without him even saying it.

He pulls me into him and I rest my head on his chest again, my eyes returning to the view below us. Jay rests his chin on top of my head. I swear I could stay here forever. Well, my legs might give out at some point, and I'm pretty sure I'd need to use the ladies room in the near future. But for now, I'm just going to pretend like I could do this forever.

"I don't think I want this to end," Jay says out loud what I'd just been thinking.

"Me either," I say.

"Maybe ..." he pauses, uncertainty in his voice. "Maybe it can be a beginning."

"I'd like that," I say, feeling my pulse start to race as my hormones high-five each other. Jay lets out a heavy breath, like he'd been holding it, waiting for me answer.

"So if this is the beginning, maybe you should tell me your first name," I say.

"My first name?" he asks, confused.

"Yeah, I saw you had an initial before your name on your credit card."

"Did you steal my wallet?" he jokes.

"No!" I say, and pull back so I can make sure he's actually joking. "I saw it at the lounge."

"Oh that," he says and then shakes his head. "I don't think I know you well enough to tell you that."

"Jay," I chide. "I think we know each other well enough."

He leans in and kisses me on the nose. "It's Chance," he says.

"Huh?" I say, not sure I heard him correctly.

"My first name is Chance."

I take in a quick breath, Elena's last words coming to my mind. *Take a chance on chance...*

"Your first name is Chance?"

"Yes. You don't believe me?" His brow furrows. "I can show you my license if you'll give me my wallet back." He winks.

"I believe you," I say. "I just ... it's just that ..." I stammer. Chance. His name is Chance. I took a chance, with Chance.

I shake my head and chuckle, looking up at the ceiling of the Empire State Building as if I can see through it and up to heaven where I'm sure Elena is chuckling right now too.

"What is it? What's funny?" Jay asks.

I contemplate telling him, but I think I'll save that for another day. It could just be a coincidence, after all. A chance. But something's telling me it's not.

His eyes are looking to me for an answer, so I say, "It's just that I'd never peg you for a Chance."

He smiles broadly and reaches up to the back of my neck, pulling me in and kissing me again. I melt into him, feeling light and free and utterly happy for the first time in a long time.

Here's to taking chances.

THE END

Made in the USA
Columbia, SC
22 November 2019